GIRLS
LIKE ME

GIRLS LIKE ME

Kristin Butcher

orca soundings

ORCA BOOK PUBLISHERS

Library and Archives Canada Cataloguing in Publication

Title: Girls like me / Kristin Butcher.
Names: Butcher, Kristin, 1951– author.
Series: Orca soundings.

Description: Series statement: Orca soundings

Identifiers: Canadiana (print) 20190069740 |
Canadiana (ebook) 20190069767 | ISBN 9781459820555 (softcover) |
ISBN 9781459820562 (PDF) | ISBN 9781459820579 (EPUB)

Classification: LCC PS8553.U6972 G55 2019 | DDC jc813/.54—dc23

Library of Congress Control Number: 2019934033
Simultaneously published in Canada and the United States in 2019

Summary: In this high-interest novel for teens, sixteen-year-old
Emma is raped by a popular boy from school.

*Orca Book Publishers is committed to reducing the consumption
of nonrenewable resources in the making of our books. We make
every effort to use materials that support a sustainable future.*

Orca Book Publishers gratefully acknowledges the support for its
publishing programs provided by the following agencies: the Government of
Canada, the Canada Council for the Arts and the Province of British Columbia
through the BC Arts Council and the Book Publishing Tax Credit.

Cover images by Stocksy.com/Sidney Morgan (front) and
Shutterstock.com/Krasovski Dmitri (back)

ORCA BOOK PUBLISHERS
orcabook.com

Printed and bound in Canada.

22 21 20 19 • 4 3 2 1

For girls and women everywhere—
you are stronger than you know.

Chapter One

The pain comes in waves. So does the blood—so much blood. My once-sky-blue sheets are now ax-murderer red.

There is a knock on my bedroom door. Before I can make myself answer, my mother is beside my bed. "Ed!" she screams. "Call an ambulance!"

I can't wait for it. I pass out, and the first responders arrive without my noticing. I miss the ride to the hospital too—the reckless weaving through the streets, the sirens wailing and lights flashing, the other vehicles diving for the curb to get out of the way. Inside the ambulance, the paramedics do whatever it is paramedics do, and though I am the one they are doing it to, I am unaware.

I don't remember arriving at the hospital either—only the vague blip of lights whizzing past overhead and voices talking around me. I wonder if I'm dying, and then I lose consciousness again.

When I truly wake up, I have to blink the world into focus. I am lying in a hospital bed, looking up at the ceiling. I turn my head and see that my arm is attached to some kind of machine. On my other side, a pouch of clear liquid hangs from a pole. A long, skinny tube snakes its way from it to my wrist.

I'm groggy, and my stomach hurts. I feel like a wrung-out dishrag.

My mother is there. She jumps up from a chair and presses her worried face against mine.

"Oh, Emma. Emma," she says, clutching my hand. Finally she pulls away and looks at me hard. I can tell she is trying to understand.

Then I see my father standing at the end of the bed. He's holding two cardboard cups of coffee. He sets them down on the tray table stretching across my legs and hurries to the other side of the bed. Ignoring the monitor on my finger, he takes my hand in both of his.

"Oh, baby," he says. "Thank god you're all right. Your mother and I have been worried sick."

I smile. At least, I try to. But the muscles in my face have seized up, and nothing much happens. "Sorry," I say. The word comes out as a croak, so I try again. The second effort is no better than the first.

My father pats my hand, as if to say he understands, but I know he doesn't.

"You women and your female troubles," he says awkwardly.

He has no clue.

But my mother does. Though she smiles at my dad's lame joke, her grip on my hand tightens. Oh yeah. She knows.

The doctor keeps me in the hospital overnight, but I am released the next morning. My parents take me home.

I enter my bedroom cautiously, half expecting to see the previous day's horror. But there's not a trace. My mother has taken care of it, and the room is as pristine as it has been my whole life. It looks exactly the same—right down to the blue sheets on the bed. New ones.

The old ones will be in the trash. Not even my mother could clean away that much blood. And she would want all evidence of what happened gone.

It is a quiet day. My parents and I retreat to our corners, avoiding awkward conversation. My mother stays in the kitchen with her pots and pans, ignoring the fact that she's making enough food to feed the neighborhood. My father holes up in his man cave, watching football with the sound turned way down. I hide in my bedroom, pretending to read.

I've just lived through a six-week nightmare, capped off with twenty-four hours of pure hell. Even so, I am still having trouble getting my head around everything. This kind of stuff doesn't happen to girls like me.

Except that it did.

I'm barely three months into eleventh grade, and the year is already unforgettable—for all the wrong reasons.

It started when Jen and I both made the senior girls' volleyball team. The two of us have been joined at the hip since kindergarten—Brownies, gymnastics, tennis lessons, summers at the lake, lemonade stands—we've done all of it together. We even kid around that one day we'll marry twins and have a double wedding. So we kind of expected that if one of us made the team, the other would too.

For a while it was great. The schedule for the senior girls was the same as for the senior boys, so game days were like a big party. After the matches everyone would meet up at a fast-food place for a few laughs before heading home.

Then something happened. Jen and I both fell for Ross Schroeder. He's the power hitter on the boys' volleyball team. And he's in twelfth grade. He has it all—a jock with good looks, smarts and personality. Every girl in school thinks he's hot, so why not Jen and me?

At first we laughed about it. I mean, it figures we would fall for the same guy, right? However, it soon became clear that neither one of us was going to back off. That's when things got a little tense, especially when Ross was around. But the day he picked up the tab for my food at the restaurant, our friendship was over.

Jen and I were standing in line behind him.

"Root beer, not cola—right?" he said to me.

My stomach flipped. I was flattered that he'd noticed what drink I liked. I nodded.

"Fries?"

I smiled and nodded again, reaching into my pocket for money. He shook his head.

"This one's on me, Emma."

"Thanks," I said. I waited for him to ask Jen what she wanted.

When he didn't, I could almost see the wall going up between us. She didn't even sit with Ross and me, and as soon as she was done eating, she left.

Despite having the coolest guy in school all to myself, I felt like a heavy rock had just dropped into my stomach.

"There goes my ride," I said, as I watched Jen's car pull out of the parking lot. "I better call my dad."

"Don't worry about it," Ross said. "I can give you a lift home."

A quiet tap on my bedroom door jerks me out of the memory. I look up from the page I've been staring at ever since I opened the book.

My mother pokes her head into the room. "Supper's on the table," she says. "Lasagna—your favorite." Then her head disappears. But in a second it's back again. "Oh, and Emma, I think it would be best if you stayed home from school tomorrow. Give your body a bit more time to recover." She shrugs. "You know."

I want life to be normal again, and that includes school. So I say, "Honestly, Mom, I'm fine. I'm just a little tired. All I need is a good night's sleep."

She shakes her head. "Missing one day is not going to affect your school-work. I think it's best. You can use the time to book a follow-up appointment with the doctor."

I bite the inside of my lip. Visiting old Dr. Abernathy is the last thing I want to do. I saw how he looked at me in the hospital. The only reason he didn't start preaching right then was because my parents were there. Behind the closed door of his office, I won't be so lucky.

"You need to talk to him," my mother says.

Why? I almost blurt. *What's there to talk about?*

I was pregnant, and now I'm not. I don't even want to think about it, never mind talk about it. Nobody was supposed to find out. But now Dr. Abernathy knows, and so does my mother— even though she hasn't come right out and said anything.

I squeeze my eyes shut and wish myself anywhere but where I am.

When I open them again, I'm still sitting on my bed, and my mother is still watching me.

"Supper's getting cold," she says and heads back to the kitchen.

Chapter Two

I wake up to the beep of my parents'
alarm clock, but I'm not ready to take
on the world. It isn't until I hear the
garage door open and close that I peel
back the covers and sit up. Even then,
I listen hard for a couple of minutes to
be sure I'm alone before shoving my
feet into my slippers and heading for
the bathroom.

As I turn on the water, I study my face in the mirror. Despite all that's happened, I look like I always look. Almost. All my parts are there, but it's like they've been cut from a photograph and pasted on. It takes a while for me to realize why that is. And then it hits me. The dead feeling weighing me down on the inside has spread to my outside. I'm as flat as stale soda pop.

I sigh. It's a good thing I'm not going to school today. One look at me, and everyone would know something is wrong. I smile at my reflection, but it doesn't smile back. So I chuck a towel at the mirror and make my way to the kitchen.

There's a note from my mother stuck to the fridge, reminding me to call Dr. Abernathy's office. As if I'd forget.

I pour a glass of orange juice and lean against the counter as I drink it. A package of frozen ground beef sits on a plate in the spotless, stainless-steel sink. With my fingernail, I scratch an unhappy face into the frost on top and wonder how my mother plans to transform it into supper. Not that it matters.

Nothing matters.

I shake my head in wonder. Two days ago everything mattered. I was one gigantic, jangled nerve, walking an emotional tightrope along the edge of the world. But no matter how carefully I stepped, I knew I was never going to make it to the other end. Then suddenly I wasn't pregnant anymore, and my problems were gone.

Sort of.

Now all I feel is numb.

I make some toast, take it into the family room and switch on the television. At this time of day, it's soap-opera city, which means I can park my worries and lose myself in other people's troubles for a few hours.

It almost works too. No one is being raped, getting pregnant or having an abortion. There's just the usual adultery, embezzlement, lies and deadly diseases that viewers seem to crave. It isn't until the commercials come on that I'm slammed back into reality.

It's just a freaking ad for diapers, but suddenly I'm sobbing like crazy, and tears are streaming down my cheeks. I am shocked. I so didn't see this coming. Probably because it's the first time I've cried since Ross...I scowl and swipe at my tears. Even though it's been almost two months, I still can't look at that memory head on.

Ross's face pops into my head, and I shudder. I can't believe how attracted I was to him when I got into his car that night, and how—just a half hour later—I completely hated him.

And myself too. I hadn't stopped him, and I may never be able to forgive myself for that. Not that I didn't try. I did. I told him *no*. I pushed him away. I screamed. I hit him. But none of it did any good. We were parked where no one could hear me. And he had me cornered before I even realized what was happening. He was bigger and stronger, and he pinned me down as easily as if I were a rag doll. I have never felt so helpless in my life.

If only I hadn't accepted his offer to drive me home.

How I wish I could turn back the clock. If I had called my dad, life would be like it was before—how it's supposed to be. I would still be me. I wouldn't have been forced to have sex. I wouldn't have gotten pregnant. I wouldn't have...

A ragged breath escapes me, and the tears start to gush again.

I fly off the couch, swiping at my eyes with my sleeve. There's no point having a pity party. It won't make me feel less guilty or ashamed. Nothing can do that. Besides, it's probably hormones making me emotional. Once my body gets back to normal, I'll be fine.

That thought reminds me that I need to make the appointment with Dr. Abernathy. I glance at the clock. It's after ten. His office will be open now. I stomp to the kitchen and grab the phone off the counter. I'll feel better once I've got this over with.

I don't. Though the receptionist is polite and businesslike, I can't help thinking she's judging me.

"May I ask the reason for the appointment?" she says.

I'm momentarily stunned. I hadn't expected to have to explain.

"It's personal," I tell her.

"Are you wanting a physical exam?" she prods.

"No," I reply quickly. That's the last thing I want. I try to come up with an explanation that will get her off my back. "I was in the hospital recently," I say, "and Dr. Abernathy wants to follow up."

"I see," she replies. "Right then. How does Thursday morning sound? Will ten thirty work for you?"

"That's fine," I mumble, scribbling down the day and time. "Thanks." I punch the Off button.

I return the phone to its cradle and wait for it to ring—my mother checking to see if I've made the appointment. She *will* call. It's just a matter of when. But I don't want to talk to her, so I head to the shower.

It's an ugly day—overcast and blustery—but I feel trapped inside the house. I put on my coat and hat and head out. At the end of the driveway, I turn left and let the wind push me down the street.

I have no idea where I'm going. I walk aimlessly, hoping to distract myself from my thoughts. But they walk right along with me.

I know Dr. Abernathy is going to give me the third degree on Thursday. How much is a doctor allowed to poke into a patient's personal life? I try to figure out what questions he'll ask and how I'll answer them.

He already knows I didn't go to an abortion clinic. I would have. In fact, I'd just about talked myself into it when— well, when Mother Nature took care of things for me.

I guess I was lucky. If you call having a miscarriage lucky. I'm not sure how I feel about that. I didn't want to be pregnant, but in a way I'm sad that I lost the baby. I know that doesn't make sense, but nothing about my life makes sense anymore. I kick a pine cone across the sidewalk and pick up my pace.

Will Doctor Abernathy ask about the father? Not that the word *father* even belongs in the same sentence with Ross Schroeder. I did consider telling him I was pregnant—for about a millionth of a second.

The thing is, I considered having the baby. I figured I could quit school and get a job. But what kind of job? Waitress? Office receptionist? Certainly nothing that paid well enough to live on, let alone support a baby. I wouldn't even be able to afford diapers. I pictured myself homeless. What kind of life was that?

Giving up the baby wasn't the answer either. I would wonder about it for the rest of my life.

Over and over I considered the options, but nothing had seemed right. Keeping the baby or giving it up— either way I would have had to tell my parents. The mere thought made me want to throw up.

No matter how much I thought about things, I couldn't make a decision. All I was doing was running in circles. And time was ticking away.

Then—just like that—the problem solved itself.

And now it's all over. So why can't I stop thinking about it?

A fat raindrop splats on the sidewalk, then another and another. I look up at the dark sky. In a matter of seconds, my face is soaked. Rain or tears—I can't tell. I turn back into the wind and start for home.

Chapter Three

The next morning I spend ten minutes searching my closet for just the right outfit. Something invisible. Not invisible clothes. I mean clothes that will make *me* invisible. Until my life gets back on track, I need to fade into the background.

I settle on a pair of jeans and a hoodie. That's the uniform of at least half the kids at school. If anything can make me blend in, it's that.

I arrive at school just before the bell. Most everybody has already made their way to their first-period classes, and the halls aren't completely empty but close to it. Invisibility plan still working.

No one is near my locker, so I quickly dial my combo. I have just enough time to hang up my jacket, grab my books and get to math before the bell rings. My timing couldn't have been better. I slide into my seat just as Mrs. Frome shuts the door. She takes attendance, the loudspeaker on the wall spouts the morning announcements, and class gets underway.

Mrs. Frome introduces the lesson, gives us our assignment and then walks up and down the aisles to see how everyone is doing.

And that's when things go sideways. When she gets to me, she lowers herself onto her haunches—probably not easy for an overweight fifty-year-old woman to do—and looks me directly in the eyes.

"How are you feeling, Emma?" she whispers.

"Fine," I say. Why is she asking me that? And why does she look so concerned? It's not like I've been away from school for weeks with mono or hepatitis. I've only missed one day.

She nods and smiles. "I understand," she says.

What is that supposed to mean? I'm starting to feel very uncomfortable. Our little chat is attracting stares from the other kids.

She pats my hand. "Well, if you have to leave the room for any reason, don't feel you need to ask for permission. Just slip out quietly. I'll understand."

There's that understanding bit again. Exactly what is it that she understands?

She grabs onto my desk with both hands and hauls herself back to a standing position. Then she glances at the clock on the wall, and in her official teacher voice she says, "Five more minutes, people, and then we'll take up the assignment."

I turn back to my work and try to concentrate on algebra. But I'm gripping my pencil so tightly and pressing so hard on the paper that the lead snaps off and flies into space.

"Great," I mutter and head for the pencil sharpener. When I get back, I see a folded paper on my open textbook. A note? From whom? I look around the room for a clue, but everyone is focused on their work.

I lower the paper into my lap and open it. It's a crude stick drawing of a guy and a girl doing it. There's a word bubble coming from the guy's grinning face. *How 'bout it?* it reads.

An icy wave rolls through me, and I suddenly feel sick. I want to run and hide. But I know that whoever sent that note is watching, and I won't—I *can't*—fall apart. It takes all the willpower I possess, but I keep my face blank, slip the paper into my backpack and return to the assignment. I write down whatever numbers shoot out the end of my pencil.

I may seem calm on the outside, but inside it's chaos. Why would someone send me that rude drawing? Has Ross been bragging to his friends? Does the whole school know what happened? I'm so mortified, I want to die.

When the class finally ends, I think about bolting for home, but I can't hide for the rest of my life. So I tell myself the vulgar note was a one-off from a stupid jerk who doesn't matter, and I head for geography class.

It goes okay. There are no more incidents. Third class is fine too. Looks like I was letting myself get all worked up over one pathetic moron. Just forty minutes more and the morning will be done. I'll have half a day behind me. The thought cheers me up, and I make my way to English.

But I'm not even in my seat when I spot the graffiti scribbled on my desk in bright green ink. Nothing unusual about that, except that this graffiti is about me. *For fun and games, call Emma*—and my phone number. Though I'm horrified, I try not to show it. Casually I set my books on top of the graffiti and sit down. I'm tempted to check my cell for messages, but I don't dare. If there are replies to the graffiti—and I pray there aren't—I prefer to see them on my time, without an audience.

When the bell rings for lunch, I stay behind, pretending I need help with my essay. The truth is, I want to scrub the graffiti off my desk. I also want to avoid the crowds in the hall. My strategy works, because by the time I get to my locker, everyone has either left the building or made their way to the cafeteria.

I retrieve my lunch, shut my locker—and stop. Where am I going? Definitely not to the crowded caf. And it's too cold to eat outside. I start down the hall. Maybe I can find an empty classroom. The second door I try is unlocked, so I let myself in.

Though I'm grateful to have found temporary refuge, the situation feels wrong. I'm a social person. At least, I was before Ross messed up my life.

I shouldn't be sitting by myself in an empty classroom. I should be in the cafeteria with Jen and my other friends.

But things between Jen and me changed the instant Ross showed interest in me. I wanted to tell her what happened that day, but I couldn't. She was already upset, and I was afraid she wouldn't understand. By the time I realized I was pregnant, our relationship was so strained I wasn't even sure she'd be on my side. So I didn't say a word. Every day we drifted farther apart. Now we don't hang out at all or even phone each other. And even though our lockers are side by side, we barely talk at school. We didn't have an argument. We just stopped being friends.

I hear the classroom door handle jiggle, and I spin toward it just as a girl walks in. When she sees me, she stops.

It's Gwen Robson. She's in my geography class.

"Sorry," she says. "I didn't know anyone was in here. Can I come in? I just had a fight with my boyfriend, and I don't want to talk to him right now. I don't think he'll look for me in here."

I shrug. The last thing I want is company, but I can't very well tell her to leave.

For a few minutes we eat our lunches in silence. It's Gwen who finally speaks.

"You weren't in geography class yesterday."

I shake my head. "Did I miss anything important?"

"Not really. Were you sick?"

"Nothing contagious," I say.

She smiles. "Oh, I'm not worried about that. I almost never get sick. My mom says I have the constitution of a horse."

I don't even try to return her smile. My face doesn't do that anymore. I just nod and take another bite of my sandwich.

She changes the subject. "My boyfriend can be such a jerk. Sometimes I think I should break up with him and find someone else." When I don't reply, she adds, "Do you have a boyfriend?"

It's none of her business, but I can't be bothered to tell her so. Instead I shake my head again. "No."

"You *were* going out with Ross Schroeder though, weren't you?"

That catches me off guard. "No," I say too quickly and too emphatically.

She sits forward on her chair, and her eyes bug out. "Yes, you were. You must have been. Everyone says he's the one who got you…" Her voice trails off.

"He's the one who got me *what*?" I throw the words back at her. "Flowers? Concert tickets?"

She goes red in the face and then starts speed-talking. "Forget it. I don't know what I'm saying. I must have mixed you up with someone else. Sorry."

"Right," I mutter. Who's she trying to kid? She didn't mix me up with anyone. She probably came in here to pump me for information.

I shove the remainder of my lunch into the bag and stomp out of the room.

Chapter Four

I spend what's left of the lunch hour locked in a bathroom stall, trying to calm down. If that little bomb Gwen Robson dropped is true, everyone in school thinks I'm pregnant! How can I ever show my face again? But then I have a thought. When it becomes obvious I'm *not* pregnant, whoever is spreading that rumor is the one who'll look stupid. I just have to hang on until that happens. Which could be months, I remind myself, getting wound up all over again.

That's when the bell rings, sending me into total panic. I can't go to class. Even if no one speaks to me, I'll know what they're thinking.

But I can't avoid people forever. Besides, I still have my pride. I shut my eyes and dig all the way to my toes for courage. Then I lift my chin, throw back my shoulders and head for my locker.

Jen is getting her stuff when I arrive. She'll know who's spreading the rumors. I tap her on the shoulder. She spins around, banging her hand on the locker door and dropping the book she's holding.

"Ow!" she cries as she bends to pick it up. "What the hell, Emma?"

"Why are people talking about me?"

She raises an eyebrow. "As if you don't know."

"If I knew, I wouldn't be asking," I snap. I grab her arm. "I know you know, Jen. Tell me." When she still doesn't answer, I add, "I thought you were my friend."

"And I thought you were mine," she snarls and pulls her arm free. "Looks like we were both wrong." She turns back to her locker. "I have to get to class."

"Please, Jen," I say. "Ever since Ross paid for my food that night after volleyball, you've been mad at me. I get it, but I never meant for him to get in the way of our friendship. I swear. It just sort of happened. If he'd picked you instead, you would have done the same as me."

She whirls around again. "Have sex with him the very first time he looked at me? I don't think so, Emma."

She might as well have reached out and slapped me. Her words have the same effect. "It…it wasn't like that," I protest weakly.

But now that Jen has unleashed her anger, it keeps right on coming. "Oh, please. Stop pretending you're innocent. The whole school knows how easy you are. The fact that you got pregnant and then lost the baby is pretty much proof, don't you think?"

I stagger backward. I'm too stunned to deny the accusation. "How can people possibly know that?"

Jen seems surprised by my response. "So it's true then."

"Who's saying this?" I demand.

She shakes her head. "I thought I knew you, but I guess I was wrong."

"Who told you?" I ask for the third time, my voice shrill in my ears.

"If you must know—Deena Watson. She's told everybody. Her older brother is an orderly at the hospital. He was there when the ambulance brought you in Saturday night. He heard a nurse say you'd had a miscarriage."

Suddenly I feel totally exposed. I might as well be standing in the middle of the hallway naked. I squeeze my eyes shut and pray for the floor to open up and swallow me, or for the ceiling to crash down on my head. When I open my eyes again, Jen is gone.

By the time I drag myself out of my stupor, the halls are empty and the classroom doors are closed. The bell must have rung, but I didn't hear it. It doesn't matter. I have no intention of going to class anyway.

I dial in my combination and tug open the locker door. As I reach for my coat, a couple of papers slide off the shelf and flutter to the floor. I pick them up. I've never seen them before, and I have no idea how they got into my locker.

One is a porn photo. The other is a religious flyer, urging me to find God and save myself.

I look from one to the other in disbelief. Is this torture ever going to end? I crumple to the floor in a broken heap. I'm not even seventeen years old, and my life is ruined. I bury my head in my arms and let the hurt pour out.

"Get up, Emma. Come on. Come with me."

I look up through my tears. Everything is a blur, but I know there's someone bending over me. The gentle voice murmuring comforting words belongs to Mrs. Hargrove, the school counselor. But where did she come from? And when? I blink to clear my vision. I don't even know how long I've been sitting on the floor.

"Come on," she says again, sliding an arm under my elbow and pulling me to my feet. She grabs my coat and drapes it over my shoulders. Then she closes up my locker and leads me down the hall to her office. She eases me into a chair and pushes a box of tissues across the desk. Then she opens a bottle of water and sets it down beside the tissues.

"Now," she says, as she pats my hand and pulls up another chair, "you can have yourself a good cry in private. No one will bother you here. And when you're done—if you feel up to it—we can talk."

I should try to pull myself together. Apologize for causing a fuss. Tell Mrs. Hargrove I'm fine. Take my coat and leave. But I don't do any of those things. I haven't stopped crying since Mrs. Hargrove found me at my locker. The thing is, I don't think I could stop even if I tried. And it's too late to be

Kristin Butcher

embarrassed. So I grab a handful of tissues and continue to bawl.

I run out of tears before I run out of hurt. It goes right on twisting inside me like a corkscrew. My eyes are sore and puffy, and my eyelashes are stuck together. Whatever makeup I had on is long gone. My face is hot, and my nose is running. I give it a good long blow.

"Thank you, Mrs. Hargrove," I say as I drop the used tissues into the waste-basket. I sound as if I have the worst cold ever. "I feel much better now." I stand up and take some more tissues. "I should go." I don't actually feel any better, and I have no idea where I'm going, but I can't stay here.

Mrs. Hargrove waves me back into the chair and taps the bottle of water. "You sound like you've been eating sand. Have some water."

I do as she says and take a sip. I am surprised at how it soothes my throat.

"Good." She nods. "Now, why don't you tell me what has you so upset. Maybe I can help."

I thought I was out of tears, but one trickles down my cheek. *Damn!* I shouldn't have had that water. I brush the tear away. "You've been so nice." I sniff. "And I'm grateful. Really. But I'm fine." I stand up again. "I should go."

She offers me an encouraging smile. "Are you sure? You don't look fine. You know, sometimes even just talking can help."

I shake my head. "I can't." Mrs. Hargrove seems like she genuinely wants to help, and I so want to tell her the whole horrible story, but I don't dare. She's the school counselor. I know that if she even suspects a student has been abused, she has to report it. I can't risk that.

Still...I could tell her it happened to a friend. I discard the idea before I've even finished thinking it. She'd see right through that. Nobody falls to pieces over someone else's problem.

"It's my boyfriend," I blurt. Why did I say that? Now I'm going to have to explain.

Mrs. Hargrove nods to the chair but doesn't say anything.

I should shut my mouth and leave, but I sit back down. My brain is spinning a million miles a minute. What should I say now?

"We broke up," I lie. "He wanted to do it, but I didn't." That part's not a lie, though there's more to it.

"I see," Mrs. Hargrove says. "That's obviously upset you very much. If you want to talk about it, I'm here to listen."

Despite her assurances, part of me says, *Don't do it!* Even though I wouldn't be telling the whole truth, it would be too close for comfort, and I might slip up. But another part of me—the frightened, lost and desperate part, the part that's weary of going it alone and wants to be rescued—is hopeful.

So I crack the lid on my box of secrets and let a few of them trickle out.

Chapter Five

I don't tell Mrs. Hargrove what really happened, but I find sharing even part of the truth is a relief. I don't mention Ross by name, and I don't say he forced himself on me. I just say I wasn't comfortable with how things were going and worried about next time. So I broke up with him.

"I know it doesn't feel like it now," Mrs. Hargrove says, "but I think you made a wise decision. Chances are, he would have been more insistent next time. And if he forced you, that would be rape."

Hearing the word makes me wince.

"Yes, Emma. Rape. The thing that makes it so terrible is that it is as much about power as it is about sex." She pauses and then adds, "It's a criminal offense."

I pull back in shock.

She puts a hand on my arm, and my blood pressure comes down a notch. "And it's not generally a one-time thing. A guy who rapes once will probably do it again. It sounds like you had a lucky escape."

"I guess," I say. "But what if I hadn't?" The second the question leaves my mouth, I want to bite it back.

Mrs. Hargrove looks at me for what seems a very long time. Finally she says, "But you did." It's more a question than a statement. "Even so, the situation has clearly upset you. It might be a good idea to talk to a trauma counselor. I could make the arrangements."

I quickly shake my head. "No, no. I'm good. Really. I was just feeling sorry for myself." I shrug. "You know—about breaking up with my boyfriend. I wasn't sure I'd done the right thing. But now I see that I did. Like you said, I was lucky."

She frowns but nods. "Okay. That's good. But you realize that girls who aren't as lucky should talk to the police."

My stomach does a somersault. There's no way I can go to the police. I've seen the shows on television, and I've read the newspaper. People always think it's the girl's fault—that somehow she asked for it. And if my dad found out what happened, I would just die.

The bell rings, announcing class change, and I shoot Mrs. Hargrove a panicked *you're not going to make me go* look.

"Why don't you take the rest of the afternoon off?" she says. "I'll check you out at the office. Tomorrow morning you'll come back to school and make a fresh start, get on with your life."

I know Mrs. Hargrove means well, but I can't bear the idea of ever facing the kids at school again. They all know—or think they know—what I've done.

"But I'm so embarrassed," I mumble. "People saw me crying. I just know they're going to be talking about me."

"There's nothing you can do about gossip," Mrs. Hargrove says. "It hurts, but you can tough it out. You're strong enough to live through it. Besides, it won't last. In a day or two you'll be yesterday's news, and the gossip mongers will have moved on to something—or someone—else." She squeezes my hand. "You're a good person, Emma Kennedy. Remember that. Don't let anyone bully you into believing differently. Hold your head high."

I nod and try to smile, although inside I'm panicking. It's easy for Mrs. Hargrove to give me a pep talk. She isn't the one everyone will be staring at and whispering about.

"I'll go to class tomorrow," I say, "but I'm not going to volleyball after school." I start to say, *The guy who raped me*, but catch myself. "My ex-boyfriend is on the boys' team."

"You shouldn't give up doing what you enjoy. Seeing him could be uncomfortable, but you can avoid him. Stay close to your team and leave right after your match."

"Yeah, I guess. But I don't have a ride to the game. I usually go with someone on my team, but we're kind of not talking at the moment."

"Don't worry. I'll find you a ride. You just be ready to play." As I stand to leave, she adds, "And Emma, my door is always open. If you want to talk some more or just need a shoulder to cry on— any time—I'm here."

Mrs. Hargrove is right about people losing interest in me. At school the next day, there are no notes or dirty pictures in my locker, no graffiti anywhere and, as far as I can tell, no one leering at me. In fact, aside from a few curious glances, nobody even seems to see me. I've gone from living under a spotlight to being invisible. Overnight. It's weird, but it's also a huge relief.

As for volleyball, Mrs. Hargrove has arranged for me to ride with Kelly Vale. Though Kelly and I are both on the volleyball team, I don't really know her.

"Did Mrs. Hargrove tell you I'll be leaving right after the game?" she says, aiming the remote at her car. It beeps, and the taillights flash.

"Yeah. I was hoping to get home right after, so that's good," I reply, opening the passenger door. The seat is covered with fast-food cups and wrappers.

"Sorry about that," Kelly says, sliding behind the wheel. "Just dump them on the floor."

I sweep the junk off the seat and onto a pile of even older garbage. There's barely room for my feet, but I squeeze in and buckle up.

"I'm not really part of the in-crowd," Kelly says. "That's why I never hang around after games."

"You're not missing anything," I tell her, although a couple of months ago I would never have said that. Back then I was proud to be part of the popular crowd.

"You have Mrs. Frome for math?" Kelly asks.

"Uh-huh."

"What's she like? I get her next term, and I need to get a decent mark. The thing is, math isn't my best subject. I need a teacher I can really understand."

"She's okay," I say. "I'm not a math whiz either, and I'm getting 81 percent. If you get stuck, maybe I can help."

She smiles. "Thanks. I may take you up on that."

We talk easily the rest of the way. Kelly seems nice, and she never once says anything to imply she knows about my situation. That lifts my spirits a little. Maybe the whole world isn't judging me after all.

The girls play first, and we win our match easily. Though I'm usually a starter, the coach doesn't sub me in until the second game. I can't help wondering if he's heard the rumors about me and is being cautious because of my recent "condition."

Of course, the guys are in the bleachers, cheering us on. I try not to look at Ross, but I can't help it. He must have heard the gossip. So as casually as I can, I glance in his direction once in a while during the match. The thing is, I never once see him looking back. He only has eyes for Jen. I can tell it's not her volleyball skills he's interested in.

After the match he heads straight for her and gives her a hug. Jen hugs him back. Then they talk for a few minutes, laughing and finding reasons to touch. It's easy to see what's going on. It's the mating dance for sure.

When Ross finally moves onto the court for his match, Jen turns toward me, like she knew all along I was watching.

She smiles the smile of someone who thinks she's won.

My heart drops into my shoes, and not because I'm jealous.

Chapter Six

I watch Jen and some other girls from my team climb into the stands. Later they'll go to some fast-food joint with the guys. Not long ago I was part of that crowd. It's strange to be on the outside looking in, and I can't deny I feel a twinge of envy. But then Ross passes through my line of vision, and my heart hardens.

"Ready to go?" Kelly says as she fishes her keys out of her gym bag.

I force a smile. "All set."

I know we chat on the drive home, but when she drops me in front of my house, I can't remember a single thing we talked about. My brain must have been on autopilot.

The only thing on my mind is Jen and Ross. They were flirting in the gym, and I'd bet anything they step it up a notch when the teams go for something to eat. I don't even want to think about what could happen after that. Thank goodness Jen has her own car. At least Ross won't be driving her home. Hopefully that means she's safe—for today anyway. But if what Mrs. Hargrove said about guys like Ross is true, it's just a matter of time until he takes advantage of her like he did me.

I have to warn her.

I worry for Jen most of the evening and into the night. The thought that she could be Ross's next conquest makes me feel sick. I don't want her to go through what I went through—what I'm still going through. It's over, but I can't seem to get past it. *Will I ever?* I try to convince myself that I'm jumping to conclusions. Ross might not even try anything. *Yeah, right.*

When morning finally arrives, I feel like a bag of dirt. I look like one too. But at least I've made a decision. I can't stop Jen from going out with Ross. But I can tell her what he did to me.

My confession is going to have to wait until the afternoon, though, because this morning I am meeting Dr. Abernathy.

I hop on the bus heading downtown. I push my concern for Jen to the back of my mind and start worrying about what the doctor is going to say.

Dr. Abernathy has been my doctor my whole life, but I've never liked him. Every visit feels like a test. One that I never quite pass. When I was eight, I got bronchitis and missed a whole week of school. I thought he would be sympathetic, but all he did was talk about the importance of washing my hands and keeping my coat zipped. It was more of the same when I fell off my bike and broke my arm. As he was putting the cast on, he lectured me about bicycle safety and the rules of the road. Every single time I see him, I come away feeling like it's my fault for getting sick or injured. I don't imagine today will be any different.

As I ride the elevator to the fifth floor, I study my blurred reflection in the stainless-steel walls. Even out of focus I look awful. I comb my hair with my fingers, pinch my cheeks and stand up straighter.

The doors open onto a long hall with a blue-patterned carpet. Dr. Abernathy's office is directly across the way, so I go through the door and let the receptionist know I'm here. I consider hanging up my coat but decide against it. I might want to make a quick exit. There are two other people in the dimly lit waiting room, one at each end of a row of armless chairs lining the wall. I grab a magazine and take a seat halfway between them.

I've barely started flipping the pages when the receptionist calls my name. "Emma Kennedy? The doctor will see you now."

I'm surprised. Though I'm right on time for my appointment, there are patients ahead of me.

"But—" I gesture to them.

The receptionist waves away my objection. "Mrs. Murray is waiting for her husband, and Mr. Dockery is early. You're next."

I take the magazine with me. Good thing, too, because it's another ten minutes before Dr. Abernathy shows up.

When he finally arrives, he's carrying a file folder with my name on it. He shuts the door, sits at the desk and opens the folder.

I hold my breath.

Eventually he looks up. I think maybe he'll smile to break the ice. But no. My mother would say his expression shows concern. I say it smacks of disapproval. He's definitely frowning.

"How are you feeling?" he says.

I shrug. "Okay."

"No more heavy bleeding or cramping?"

"No."

"Any fever? Fainting? Nausea?"

"No."

"How about mood swings?"

"Sometimes I get a little emotional, but it doesn't last."

"That's normal," he mutters into the folder.

He studies its contents in silence for another minute or so, then turns his full attention on me. Under his unwavering gaze, I feel self-conscious.

"How old are you, Emma?"

"Sixteen," I say. "I'll be seventeen in a couple of months."

"And you have a boyfriend."

"No."

He raises an eyebrow. "But you're sexually active."

Bam! I walked into that one. Now he thinks I'm a slut. "Not really," I protest meekly. "It...it was just that one time." Heat rushes into my cheeks. I look down at my hands. I want to make Dr. Abernathy understand that it wasn't my fault. That I was forced to have sex. But I'm too embarrassed to say a word.

"And you became pregnant," he says.

I feel my jaw tighten. Why does he keep stating the obvious? We both know what happened.

He opens the drawer of his desk and pulls out a handful of pamphlets. "Here." He passes them to me. "This is information on birth control. I want you to read it. If you have any questions, come back and see me."

Fat chance of that!

He turns to his computer and types something. A few seconds later the printer on the shelf beside the desk spits out two sheets of paper. He hands one to me. "This is a prescription for vitamins," he explains. "You're a bit rundown, and your body needs to build itself back up. These vitamins will help.

And this"—he holds out the second paper—"is for birth control pills. An ounce of prevention is worth a pound of cure."

I don't even want to touch the paper. *I don't need birth control pills! I'm not having sex!* I silently scream.

Then he stands, so I do too. Thank goodness we're done. The clock on the wall says our talk has taken ten minutes, but it feels like hours.

"Thank you, Dr. Abernathy," I mumble and start for the door.

He stops me. "One more thing, Emma."

I turn around.

"I don't know the specifics of your situation, and I can see that you would like to keep it that way. But I think you should talk with someone—a friend, a teacher, a counselor maybe. Of course, the best person to speak with is your mother.

She cares what happens to you as much as you do. And no one knows you better."

Horror at the mere thought of sharing this horrible experience with my mother must show on my face, because he adds, "Trust me. It will help."

Chapter Seven

On the bus ride home I replay the appointment in my head. It went pretty much as I expected—except for the birth-control prescription. I wasn't ready for that. But I understand why Dr. Abernathy assumed I needed it. A girl doesn't get pregnant by holding hands. I shove the piece of paper to the bottom of my pack and get back to worrying about Jen.

I arrive at my locker way before the start of afternoon classes. Lately I've been avoiding people, but today I have no choice. I need to talk to her. The thing is, she doesn't show. She isn't there at the end of the day either, and I wonder if she's been at school at all. I ask the girl with the locker on the other side of hers. She says Jen was there in the morning.

Maybe she went home sick or had an afternoon appointment of some kind or a field trip. I consider calling her on her cell, but what I have to say isn't something I want to share over the phone.

"So how did your appointment with Dr. Abernathy go?" Dad asks at supper.

I just about choke on my mashed potatoes.

"Ed, really." Mom clucks her tongue. "That is hardly an appropriate topic for the dinner table."

My father looks confused. "Why? I'm just asking if Emma is on the mend. I would think you'd want to know too, Miriam."

My mother starts to reply, but I jump in. "I'm fine," I say with as much enthusiasm as I can muster. "Dr. Abernathy gave me a clean bill of health—and a prescription for some vitamins. He thinks I might be a bit rundown." I want to change the subject, but I know my dad must have seen my bloody sheets. I have to explain them somehow, so I say, "The doctor said that sometimes heavy bleeding—"

"Okay, okay," he interrupts. "I don't need all the details. But you should listen to the doc, Emma. Maybe slowing down a little isn't such a bad idea."

"Oh, Ed, you heard Emma. She's fine," my mother says. "Don't make such a fuss."

Dad sighs, and that's the end of the conversation. We carry on with supper.

But it's a different story when we've finished eating. Dad takes his dessert to his man cave, and Mom and I start cleaning up. I've just begun loading the dirty plates and cutlery into the dishwasher when she says, "So what really happened with Dr. Abernathy?"

I look up and frown. "I told you. He said I'm a bit rundown, but otherwise I'm fine."

She glances toward the hall to make sure Dad is out of earshot. Then, in a hushed voice, she says, "Did he talk to you about…" She pauses. "Birth control?"

My mouth literally drops open.

Placing a finger beneath my chin, she closes it. "It's a little late to play the shocked card, Emma."

Which shocks me even more. I know my mother realized I was pregnant and that I miscarried, but I can't believe she is bringing up the subject. Until this moment she hasn't even acknowledged that anything happened.

"Well?" she prods.

It's my turn to look toward the hall. "Yes," I hiss. "He gave me a prescription for birth control pills." And suddenly I'm not sure my mother has been as tight-lipped as I'd thought. She may not have spoken to *me*, but... "Was that your idea?" I say. "Did *you* ask Dr. Abernathy to do that?"

At least she has the decency to look embarrassed. "We may have talked," she mumbles.

"About me. Behind my back," I say, forgetting to keep my voice down.

She scowls and glances toward the hall again.

"I didn't see that I had a choice. *You* clearly weren't taking precautions. Someone has to look out for you."

"I don't need to take precautions," I protest, "because I'm not having sex!"

My mother winces. "You don't have to be vulgar. And keep your voice down. If your father finds out about this, he will be very upset."

"Did you hear what I said, Mom? I'm not having sex."

She grits her teeth and closes her eyes. "Stop saying that. You were pregnant, Emma. You had to have been having—relations."

"Relations?" I hoot. "That sounds so clinical. If you can't say *sex*, why not go for *sleeping with someone, being intimate* or *making love*?"

"Emma!"

I ignore her and push on. Instead of tiptoeing around the topic, we might as well get it right out in the open. "The truth is, I wasn't doing any of those things, Mom. I didn't take any precautions because I didn't have the chance. I was raped."

There. I've said it.

She doesn't gasp or spin around. She doesn't hug me or even look at me. She doesn't even stop wiping the counter, and I wonder if she's heard me.

I say it again. "A boy raped me. He forced me to have sex."

I can only see her profile, but her jaw tightens. When the counter can't get any cleaner, she tosses the dishcloth into the sink and turns to look at me. I can tell she's trying to organize her thoughts.

Finally she says, "That's a serious accusation, Emma. I understand how you might have been caught up in the heat of the moment and changed your mind when it was too late, but that's not rape."

I shake my head vehemently. "It wasn't like that. I didn't change my mind. I never wanted sex. He attacked me. He held me down. He forced me."

She puts a calming hand on my arm. "Okay. All right. Don't get all worked up. Just tell me what happened. *Where* were you?"

"In his car. He was driving me home from volleyball and stopped on a secluded road and—"

She frowns. "I thought you went to the games with Jen."

"I do. At least, I used to, but she left without me that night."

"Why would she do that?"

I lower my eyes. "Because we liked the same guy, and he was paying attention to me."

"The boy who drove you home?"

I nod.

"So did you lead him on?"

"Mother!" I squeak. "What is wrong with you? I flirted with him. Yes. But that doesn't mean I wanted to have sex."

"Well, obviously he got a different message."

I can't believe my ears. "Are you defending him?"

"No, of course not. I just think maybe you got in over your head without realizing. You're a pretty girl, and—well—you do dress provocatively sometimes, Emma. You have to know boys are going to notice."

"I don't dress any differently than other girls. And anyway, it shouldn't matter how I dress. What I wear doesn't give a guy the right to rape me! I told him no, Mom. Doesn't that count for anything?"

I can't believe we're having this conversation. Why isn't my mother sticking up for me?

She hugs me and murmurs, "Of course it counts. He was wrong. But there's not much we can do about that now. What's done is done. It's a hard lesson, but I'm sure you'll be more careful in the future and not allow yourself to end up in that situation again."

She holds me at arm's length and smiles. "You need to put it behind you, sweetheart, and get on with your life."

"That's easier said than done," I tell her. "Everyone at school is talking about me. They all know I was pregnant and that I lost the baby."

"How?"

"It doesn't matter," I say. "They just do. And it's awful."

"I'm sorry, Emma. I know that must be hard on you, but try not to think about it. In less than two years you'll be finished high school. If you work hard on your studies between now and then, it will help take your mind off what happened.

You'll be so busy you won't notice what people are saying. And it'll mean you can get into any university in the country. Then you can leave the past behind and start over."

As my mother continues to paint pictures of my future, I tune out. I don't feel her hands holding mine either. I am numb. I know she loves me and she means well, but it's as if she's lifted the corner of the living room rug and swept me and my problem under it.

Chapter Eight

Friday morning I arrive at school early to speak to Jen, but she doesn't show up until just before the bell, so there's no time. At noon my biology lab goes long, so I'm late getting to my locker. Luckily, Jen is just closing hers up, and I cut her off before she can leave.

"I need to talk to you," I say.

She frowns and attempts to go around me. I move back into her path.

She heaves an enormous sigh and rolls her eyes. "What do you want, Emma? My friends are waiting for me."

That stings. I used to be one of those friends.

"It's important," I say.

Another roll of the eyes. "Is this going to take long, because—"

I shake my head and grab her hand.

"Where are we going?"

"I need to talk to you in private," I say, pulling her into the first open classroom we come to. I shut the door and stand with my back against it.

"So now I'm a prisoner?" she says.

"I don't want anyone walking in on us."

"Fine. Get on with it then. What's the big hush-hush secret?"

"It's not a joke, Jen. Everybody in school knows I was pregnant and that I miscarried. But what only one other person besides me knows is what really happened."

"Oh, please, Emma," says Jen. "Don't be so dramatic. We all know how babies are made. I haven't got time for this." She tries to push me out of the way.

If I don't tell her about Ross right now, I may not get another chance. "I was raped," I blurt out. "It was Ross," I add.

She stops.

At first I think she's stunned and lost for words. But then she calmly shakes her head and says, "Nice try, Emma, but I already know what happened. Ross told me."

"He told you?" I'm the one who's stunned. "When?"

"Yesterday afternoon." She smirks. She's obviously enjoying my confusion.

"When?" I say again. "You weren't even at school yesterday afternoon."

"That's because I was with Ross."

"You skipped school?"

"Not that it's any of your business, but yeah, we did. We went downtown to pick up tickets to the Ed Sheeran concert next month. Ross is taking me."

"You can't go out with him," I say. "I mean it, Jen. He's dangerous. He *raped* me. He could rape you too."

"Oh, Emma, stop it. Didn't you hear what I said? Ross told me what happened between you. And if there was any raping going on, you were the one doing it. When he gave you a ride that night, he detoured onto a quiet road. He admits that. But it was because he was hoping to talk to you before taking you home. He had no intention of having sex with you. He just wanted to get to know you better. But the second he turned the car off, you climbed all over him."

I'm incredulous. "He told you that?"

She nods.

"And you believe him?"

"I admit I didn't want to at first. I mean, I've known you a long time, and I never took you for a sex maniac, but why would he lie? He didn't have to tell me anything."

"Why would *I* lie?" I say.

"To try to save your reputation. And maybe to punish Ross for getting you pregnant. But it was you who came on to him. He says he was shocked, but he's only human. So he did what any guy in that situation would do." She shrugs. "I hate to say it, Emma, but you got what you asked for. I guess you didn't count on everyone finding out. But it's too late to cry wolf now."

"That's not what happened at all," I protest. "Ross is lying, Jen. I swear. You have to believe me. I'm telling you, he raped me! And I don't want the same thing to happen to you. Please, listen to me. Hear what I'm saying. You have to stop seeing him before it's too late."

Jen grabs the door handle. The patronizing smile on her face makes me want to slap her. "I feel sorry for you, Emma. I really do. Ross Schroeder is one of the sweetest guys out there. If he was the kind of person you say he is, he would have made a move on me by now. But all he's ever done is kiss me. So if you'll excuse me, I gotta go."

I move through my afternoon classes like a robot. Good thing there's no test. I wouldn't even get my name right.

I can't stop thinking about Jen. According to her, Ross can do no wrong. I don't get it. How can she possibly take his word over mine? We've been friends forever. She has to know I wouldn't lie about something like this.

Deep down I'm sure she does know. But Ross has her under his spell, and because of that she's not thinking straight. I have to jolt her back to her senses before it's too late. But how? I'm still trying to come up with an answer when the bell rings to end the day.

My last class is in the south hall. My locker is in the north hall, so before I can go home I have to get to the other end of the school. But everyone else seems to be headed the other way, to the student parking lot. After fighting the traffic for a minute or so, I've barely moved. So I duck into a doorway and wait for the crowd to clear.

I don't see Ross until he's past me. And then—I don't know why—I take off after him. I don't stop him or try to get his attention. I just follow him— right out of the building and through the parking lot to his car.

That's when he sees me. For a split second he looks surprised, but his expression changes so quickly, I'm not sure I didn't imagine it. Now he's smiling, and it looks so genuine, anyone watching would think he was actually happy to see me.

"Hey, Emma. How's it going?" he asks as he unlocks the car door. "I heard you were sick. Nothing catchy, I hope."

Insert knife and twist. I don't give him the satisfaction of reacting. I'm just going to say what I have to say and then get as far away from him as I can. From the corner of my eye I see kids looking at us as they head to their cars. I can only imagine the rumors that will be flying around school on Monday.

But I can't worry about that now.

"Stay away from Jen," I tell him.

He laughs. Why am I not surprised?

"Why?" he asks. "Are you jealous?"

Wham! The memory of that horrible night slams into my mind with such fury, I have to fight the urge to run at him and claw his eyes out.

"Stay away from her," I repeat through gritted teeth.

He opens the car door and prepares to get in. "Jen's a big girl. She can take care of herself."

"I'm warning you, Ross. Leave her alone, or I swear I'll—"

"You'll what?" He pauses with one foot in the car and the other on the ground.

I spit back the only thing I can think of. "I'll go to the police and tell them what you did."

"And what was that?" he sneers. "Are you gonna tell them I fucked you? So what if I did? You were begging for it."

"That's a lie, and you know it."

"It's your word against mine." He shrugs. "You do what you gotta do, Emma, but everybody—including your former best friend—already thinks you sleep around. I'm not too worried."

What can I say? He's right. No one would believe me. I'd be more of a laughingstock than I already am.

I watch in mortified silence as he slides behind the wheel and starts up the engine. As the car crawls past me, he rolls down the window. "It was nice talking to you, Emma. Are you sure I can't give you a lift somewhere?"

Then he steps on the gas and burns out of the parking lot, his laughter ringing in my ears.

Chapter Nine

It's Friday night. I should be out somewhere having a good time with my
friends—if I still had friends. Instead
I'm sitting at the desk in my room, doing
homework. Homework. On a Friday
night. My mother probably thinks I've
taken her advice and am throwing
myself into my studies, so I can get into
a wonderful, faraway university.

I'm not. At least, not on purpose. And to be honest, I'm not even really doing homework. I'm just staring at my history book. My eyes have been hovering over the events leading up to World War I for a half hour, but so far nothing has made it into my brain.

How can it? Murderous thoughts of Ross Schroeder are taking up all the space there. Confronting him in the school parking lot was like reopening a festering wound, and now hate is oozing out of me like pus.

He raped me. I've spent every minute of every day since then trying to scrub the memory of that nightmare from my mind, to rewind time and reclaim my life. I'd give anything for the guilt and shame to disappear and to feel whole again.

Today was the first time I've spoken to Ross since it happened. I don't know what I was expecting. Remorse maybe?

An apology? Even an excuse. There should have been something. Anything to show he knows he did a horrible thing. That he abused my rights as a person. That he physically hurt and violated me. That he shattered my self-esteem. That he stomped all over my soul.

But there was nothing—less than nothing. Ross Schroeder expressed absolutely no remorse for what he did because he feels no remorse. After he zipped up his pants, he probably never gave me another thought.

Realizing that is like being raped all over again. Except this time, I'm not ashamed. I'm angry. And more than anything, I want Ross to feel what I feel, hurt like I hurt. If only I knew how to make that happen.

The phone rings, startling me from my vengeful thoughts. As I move to pick it up, I notice red dents in my palm where my fingernails have dug into my flesh. I didn't even realize my fists were clenched.

I glance at the screen to see who's calling, and I'm startled a second time. It's Jen. I blink at her name to be sure I'm seeing it right. My heart speeds up. Maybe our lunchtime talk had a positive effect after all. I lift the phone to my ear.

"Hello?"

"How dare you!" she screeches.

I wince and pull away from the phone. "Jen?"

"I can't believe you went to Ross behind my back!" She races on. "What gives you the right to butt into my business? Who do you think you are? You've screwed up your own life as much as you can, so now you're going to start on mine? I don't think so, Emma. Unless you want—"

"Jen!" I shout into the phone, when it's clear she has no intention of stopping her rant. "Could you listen for a second?"

There's a pause. I'm not sure if it's because she's doing what I asked or if she's merely catching her breath. No matter. It might be my only chance to speak, so I plunge ahead.

"I'm sorry. I didn't mean to butt in," I say. I have to calm her down. "I wasn't trying to run your life. I really wasn't, and I *am* sorry. Okay?"

She's clearly in no mood to be pacified. "*Okay*? Are you kidding me? No, it's not okay. It's *totally* not okay. You tail my boyfriend and tell him to stop seeing me. You have no right! None. Zip. Zero. Did you think he wouldn't tell me? What's gotten into you? You can't go around poking your nose where it doesn't belong and expect life to carry on as usual because you say you're sorry. Get real, Emma."

When she puts it that way, even I wonder how I could have done what I did. I try to explain. "I had no intention of talking to Ross. Really. It just sort of happened."

"You are such a liar!" she yells. "You followed him to his car!"

"It was a spur-of-the-moment thing. He passed me in the hall, and the memory of how he attacked me came flooding back. The next thing I knew, I was standing in the parking lot. I just wanted him to admit he'd raped me and that he lied to you about it."

Jen comes back at me so fast, I know she can't have thought about what I said. "You're the one who's lying," she shoots back. "Why can't you just face the fact that you're jealous? Ross likes me, not you, and you can't stand it. You'll resort to anything—no matter how low—to get him back."

"That's not true," I protest. "I wouldn't go near him even if he was the last guy on earth. Why won't you listen to me?"

"Because you're talking like a crazy person. You're turning into a stalker. Can't you see that? You're really starting to scare me, Emma. If you're not careful, you're going to end up in a rubber room."

I try one more time to make her see reason. "I'm not lying. And I'm not delusional. I know what Ross Schroeder did. And so does he. The thing is, he has no conscience, and he'll probably do it again—to some other girl. I just don't want it to be you."

Then I drop the phone on the desk and stare at it in amazement. I can't believe I just hung up on Jen. Not that there was any point in continuing the conversation. She was never going to believe me, no matter what I said.

Maybe that was it. If I hadn't ended the call, I would have been the one listening to dead air. At least this way, I salvage a scrap of self-respect.

Small comfort. For the millionth time I wonder how my life has become such a train wreck. The kids at school—as well as my doctor—think I'm a slut. Jen believes I'm not only a liar but have also lost my grip on reality. My mother's convinced that ignoring what happened will make it go away. And Ross Schroeder thinks the whole thing's a joke.

My life is a living hell, and all because I accepted a ride. I can't believe I was so gullible. I'm certainly not anymore—for all the good that does. I can't even keep my friend from falling into the same trap.

If only...if only...if only. I cling to those words, even though they drip acid into my gut. I feel like Prometheus from the mythology unit we're studying at school. As punishment for giving fire to mortals, he was tied to a rock and had his liver pecked out by an eagle. During the night it grew back, so he had to go through the same hell again the next day—and every day after that. His torment never ended.

Will mine?

Chapter Ten

On Tuesday the volleyball game is at our school—the last league match before playoffs—and the bleachers are filled. So, of course, the first time I touch the ball, I shank it. Then I serve it into the net—twice. When I miss a block, my coach has seen enough. He pulls me, and I ride the pine for the rest of the match. That's fine with me. Let somebody else be in the spotlight. In the last two weeks I've been stared at enough to last me a lifetime.

It's hard to believe it's only been two weeks since I was rushed to the hospital and the rumors started to fly. It feels like forever. This is shaping up to be the longest year of my life.

Somehow I make it through the week, though, and finally it's Friday again. Not that weekends are any better than school days. With only my parents and the television for company, it's not exactly a laugh a minute.

Tonight one of the guys on the boys' team is hosting a pre-playoff party. The girls' team is invited, but I don't even consider going. I still haven't recovered from my run-in with Ross, and Jen and I haven't spoken since she yelled at me over the phone. Neither one of them would want me at the party, and everyone else would treat me like I had the plague. Not a tough decision. I stay home.

There's not much on television, but I plant myself in front of it anyway. By ten o'clock I've had enough and go to bed. But I can't sleep. I spend the night flipping my pillow and fighting with my covers. When morning arrives I'm as restless as ever. I'm in a rotten mood, too, and have a terrible headache. At breakfast I force down my eggs and toast in sullen silence.

"Where are you going?" my mother asks when I show up at the front door in my sweats.

"For a run."

"It's cold out there."

I shrug. "I'm dressed in layers, and I'll be running. If anything, I'll probably end up too warm."

She eyeballs the sky through the living-room window. "It looks like it's going to rain."

I glance at her as I reach for the door-knob. "I'm pretty sure I won't shrink, Mother." Then I head outside before she can come up with any more reasons for me to stay home. She's right. It is cold, but I don't care. I'll go crazy if I stay in the house one more minute.

At the end of the driveway, I stop and breathe in the morning while I decide on a route. The air smells of burning leaves. I spy a wisp of smoke curling upward from the neighbors' yard. They must be doing a fall cleanup. I wonder if their kids bury potatoes in the fire's embers like Jen and I used to do. Those were the best baked potatoes—crusty, charred skins and crunchy, half-cooked insides that we'd slather with butter. My mouth waters, and I almost smile.

Then I feel my muscles tighten. That was then, and this is now. I push the memory aside and start to run. I don't want to think, so I concentrate on how the pounding in my head is keeping time with my feet thumping the pavement.

My plan is to go to the sports center, run a few laps around the outdoor track and then jog home again. Hopefully the exercise and fresh air will clear my head.

I have to pass Jen's place to get to the sports center, but I keep my eyes focused on the sidewalk until her house is behind me. I'm just about to turn the corner when I hear someone calling me.

"Emma!"

I glance over my shoulder. It's Jen, standing on the sidewalk in front of her house. I keep running.

"Emma, wait."

I slow down slightly, but I don't stop.

"Please, Emma! Wait!"

The desperation in her voice makes me put on the brakes and spin around.

When she catches up, I can see that she's crying, and from the look of her, she has been for quite a while. Suddenly I don't care that the last time we talked she screamed at me and called me a liar.

"What's the matter?" I say. "What's happened?"

Her answer is to break down completely, and though she's trying to speak, I can't make out a single word through her sobs. I don't know what's upset her, but it must be something pretty awful. Jen doesn't cry easily.

"Come on," I say, wrapping an arm around her shoulder. "Let's get you home."

She pulls away, her eyes bulging with fear. "No! My parents can't see me like this."

"But you're not wearing a coat," I say. "You're going to freeze out here."

"No!" She shakes her head. "Please, Emma. I can't." She looks so panicked, I don't push it.

"Fine." I nod. "We'll go to the sports center then. It's only a block away. It'll be open, and we can go inside and talk. Okay?"

"Okay."

I peel off my hoodie and offer it to her. "Put this on. It's a bit sweaty, but it's warm."

"What about you?"

"Don't worry about me," I say, pushing the top into her arms. "You're wearing a T-shirt. You've got goose bumps on your goose bumps." I snap the arm of my long-sleeved shirt. "This is thermal. I'll be fine."

We jog the block to the sports center without talking. Jen isn't crying anymore. But the second we step inside—*whoosh*—on come the waterworks again. The people standing nearby start to stare, so I steer Jen into the washroom.

Since I have no tissues, I grab a fistful of toilet paper from one of the cubicles. She swipes at her tears and blows her nose. I wet some paper towels. She wipes her face.

I wait until she's breathing normally again and then say, "So tell me what's wrong."

Tears start streaming down her cheeks again.

She's clearly hurting so much that I tear up too.

"Oh, Emma!" She can barely choke out the words. "You were right."

My body stiffens, and cold dread shoots up my spine. I know what she's going to say. A heavy metal door inside my brain slams shut. *No. Not again.*

"Ross," she squeaks. "He…he…"

I shake my head. "Shhhh." She doesn't need to say anything. I pull her into a hug, and her pain becomes mine. "It's okay, it's okay," I say as we slide down the wall to the floor. She buries her face in my shoulder, as broken as a person can be, and together we cry. "It's going to be okay." I rock her and stroke her hair. "Everything is going to be okay."

I don't know how it can be, but if I keep saying it, maybe it'll be true.

Chapter Eleven

While we sit huddled together on the washroom floor, a couple of little girls in hockey uniforms burst in, giggling. As soon as they see us, their laughter dries up. They spin back toward the door and scurry out before it's even had a chance to close.

"Come on, Jen." I drag myself to

my feet and offer her a hand up. "We can't stay here."

She stands, wipes her eyes on her sleeve and takes several deep breaths.

I reach into the pockets of my sweatpants. My phone is in one and a ten-dollar bill is in the other. I wave the money at her. "Let's get a hot chocolate. Then we can talk."

Jen's hands fly up to her face. "But I look terrible. I don't want people to see me. What will they say?"

She sounds like me, and I realize I'm past worrying about that stuff. I grab her hand and head for the exit. "Probably nothing. You find us a couple of seats away from the crowd while I get our drinks."

We end up sitting at a window overlooking an empty ice rink. Except for a kid trying to escape his mother, nobody comes near us. The hot chocolate seems to have a calming effect on Jen, because somehow she manages to tell her story with a minimum of tears. She dabs at her face once in a while with the napkins I grabbed at the canteen.

"The party was rocking. Marty Benson's parents were out for the evening, so of course the music was loud, people were dancing, laughing, talking…" She shrugs. "You know—having fun. Ross said he wanted to show me something upstairs, so I followed him. When we got to the top, he pulled me into a dark corner next to a hallway. And he kissed me."

She pauses and looks at me. "I was okay with that. I kissed him back." She closes her eyes and takes a deep breath. "And that's when everything went wrong. He kissed me again, but this time he pressed me against the wall and stuck his hand under my sweater. I tried to pull away, but I couldn't move—not my body, not my head, nothing. I was trapped.

I kind of squeaked—that's as much of a scream as I could manage. That's when I saw someone out of the corner of my eye. It was a guy, though I couldn't really see who. Ross saw him too, and without letting me go, he growled over his shoulder, *We're kind of busy here, man*."

"And the guy left?" I ask in disbelief. "He had to have noticed you were struggling."

She shrugs again. "I don't know if he did or not. But yeah, he left. And that's when Ross forced me down the hall and into a bedroom. The next thing I knew, I was lying on a bed, and he was on top of me. When I screamed, he just laughed. He said no one would hear me over the noise of the party. And even if they did, they wouldn't care. Everyone knew I was crazy about him, and they would just think we were making out."

A tear rolls down her cheek. "I didn't know what to do. I didn't know how to stop him."

I give her a hug. "I know," I say, because I do.

"Emma?"

"Uh-huh?"

"What if—what if I'm pregnant?"

I shake my head. "You're probably not."

"But what if I am?"

"Like I said, you're probably not. But if you are, you have choices. Your mom will know what to do."

She pulls away. "I can't tell my mom! I can't tell either of my parents. I'll just die if they find out! And what if Ross blabs to all his friends? The whole school will know."

I heave a huge sigh. Suddenly I'm Mrs. Hargrove, and Jen is me. I squeeze her hand. "I know you think your parents will be shocked and ashamed, Jen. But they won't be."

"You don't know that!" she wails.

"Yes, I do. You forget—I know your parents almost as well as you do. They've always been there for you no matter what. They'll be there for you now too."

As I reassure Jen, I feel a twinge of envy. I wish I could say the same about my parents. "You're not alone, Jen," I say. "Remember that. You've got me, and you have your family. You're going to get through this."

Jen and I spend another hour at the sports center. We're not even close to being talked out, but Jen's parents haven't seen her since she left for the party last night. I worry that when they realize she's not in the house, they'll call the police. Besides, I've finally convinced Jen she needs to tell them what happened. A call home is the first step. She puts the phone on *Speaker*.

"Hi, Mom."

"Jennifer, where are you? I was just going to start calling your friends. I know you came home last night. I heard you come in, but when did you leave again?"

"I'm sorry, Mom." Jen grimaces. "The thing is, something happened at the party, and it really got to me. I didn't want to talk about it, so I stayed in my room this morning. But when I saw Emma run past our house, I realized I did need to talk to someone. We're at the sports center."

"I'm sorry you're upset, honey," her mother says. "Does it have something to do with Ross?"

Jen bites her lip and tears up again. "Yes."

"Oh, honey, I'm so sorry. I'm glad you have Emma to talk to, but you can always talk to your old mom too, you know."

"I know, Mom. That's why I'm calling. I'm on my way home, and I wanted to make sure you'd be there."

When Jen hands the phone back, her hands are shaking. "Oh, Emma. I'm so scared."

"I know you are," I say. "It's natural. And it's okay. But you'll feel a lot better once you've talked with your parents." I stand up. "Come on. I'll walk you home."

Jen phones me first thing Sunday morning. She says she told her parents everything. But she still sounds worried and asks me to come over. So I wolf down a piece of toast, throw on some clothes and tear off to her house.

Her mom answers the door. Her eyes are sad and swollen, but she tries to smile and gives me a big hug. "You're a good friend, Emma Kennedy," she says, squeezing me tightly before letting go. "Jen is in her room."

I tap lightly on the door and let myself in. Jen is sitting on her bed amid a pile of used tissues. I sit beside her and give her a hug. "You okay?"

She nods. "Better than I was yesterday. You were right about my parents. They don't blame me at all. But they are really upset."

"I saw your mom," I say. "I could tell she's been crying."

Jen nods again. "We all cried— all afternoon and evening. Well, Mom and I did anyway. Dad cried too for a while, but then he got mad. He said he was going to lop off Ross's balls. He even grabbed his coat and headed for the door. I was so scared. Thank goodness Mom stopped him before he could leave. It took a lot of talking, but she finally convinced him that going after Ross wouldn't do any good."

"Oh, I don't know," I say. "Cutting off his balls would for sure stop him from raping more girls."

Jen's eyebrows shoot up, but she doesn't argue with me. "Mom's going to make a doctor's appointment for me tomorrow."

"That's good." I pat her hand.

"She thinks maybe I should see a counselor too."

"I told you your mom would know what to do."

She frowns. "My parents want me to go to the police."

There's a long pause as we both think about that. Then I ask, "Are you going to?"

Jen shuts her eyes and drags her hands down her face. "I don't know. I'm so confused—and scared. I don't want people to find out."

I nod. "I know. I feel the same." Then I have a thought. I grab her hand. "What if—" But I stop in midsentence.

"What if what?" Jen says.

I shake my head. "Never mind. It's a bad idea."

"Tell me," she insists.

"I was going to say, what if we went to the police together?"

She frowns. "What good would that do? It would just be our word against Ross's."

"But there are two of us," I point out.

"So what? We have no proof."

I sigh. She's right. I don't know what I was thinking. I've argued with myself about this so many times. How could I possibly think it would be different now just because Jen's going through the same thing?

"And if Ross got off," she continues, "we'd look like sluts and liars to the whole world."

I pound the bed with my fists. "I know. But that's so wrong! Ross is the one who's a rotten person. Not *us*!"

Then Jen completely changes the subject. "You must hate me," she says.

That catches me by surprise. "Why would I hate you?"

"Because when you needed a friend, I wasn't there. Because I didn't believe you. Because I trusted Ross instead of you."

I wave away her concerns. "Forget it. The guy is a freaking fountain of charm. He sucked us both in."

"Yeah, that's for sure. At first I thought he was a dream come true. I realized too late that he's actually my worst nightmare."

Jen is paranoid about going to school on Monday, but I remind her that nobody except Ross—and now her parents and me—actually know what happened at the party. If she acts normal, people won't suspect a thing. I don't know how much of that she buys, but she goes to class, and when we meet up at our lockers at lunchtime, she seems less stressed.

Until Ross shows up.

"Hey, Jen," he says, grinning. "Great party Friday night, don't you think? How about we get together again—say, next weekend?"

The color drains from her face, and she almost falls into her locker, trying to get away from him.

I give him a shove, but he doesn't move, and the scary memory of how he overpowered me flashes through my head. I don't let it show. "Get lost, Schroeder."

He just laughs. "Oh, Emma, don't hurt me." Then he heads for Jen again.

"I said, get lost," I growl, pushing him again—harder.

This time he shoves me back with enough force to send me stumbling into the hallway. "I'm telling you for the last time, Emma—butt out."

I fly back to the lockers, wedging myself between him and Jen. "I'll meet you in the cafeteria," I tell Jen. "Go." Then I turn my attention to Ross. I'm shaken up, but I'm angry too. "And I'm telling *you* for the last time, stay away from Jen."

He leers at me. "You threatened me before. Remember? But you've got nothing," he sneers. Then he leans in close and growls into my ear, "I, on the other hand, have plenty. If you don't start minding your own business, I'm going to tell the whole school exactly how easy you are."

"So do it," I shoot back, determined to stand up to him. "Everyone already knows you got me pregnant. The only thing they don't know is that you raped me. And you raped Jen too. I'm guessing that's the only way you can get a girl to have sex with you. Maybe everybody in school should know *that*."

"You're a big talker," he says. "But we both know you've got no backbone. You won't say a word."

As I watch him swagger down the hall, I am torn between rage and despair. I so want him to be wrong.

Chapter Twelve

When I catch up with Jen, she's standing behind the cafeteria door.

"What are you doing there?" I ask as she comes out of hiding. She looks totally stressed.

She glances uneasily toward the packed cafeteria. "I didn't want to go in alone." Then she adds, "Actually, I don't want to go in at all. Ross could've blabbed his version of what happened to someone—maybe to everyone!"

I open my mouth to tell her not to worry, but then I close it again. She has every right to be worried—and good reason too. Ross is not exactly a moral guy. As far as he's concerned, he scored with Jen. Why wouldn't he spread the word?

"Come on," I say, doing a quick turn around and heading back down the hall.

Jen hurries after me. "Where are we going?"

"To get our coats. We'll go eat somewhere else. That coffee shop on Mountain Road maybe. It's far enough away that we won't see anyone from school. You have your car, right?"

She nods.

As Jen opens her locker to get her coat, a paper flutters down from the top shelf.

"What's that?" I ask.

"I don't know." She picks it up off the floor. When she gasps, I take the paper and read it too.

I was at the volleyball party Friday night, and I saw you and Ross in the upstairs hallway. I knew you were trying to get away from him, but I thought I should mind my own business. I was wrong. I should have helped you. When I heard Ross bragging to a couple of guys after you left, I knew I'd messed up. Ross runs his mouth pretty good. You're not the first girl he's pressured into having sex. I have a sister, and if some guy did that to her, I'd want to kill him. Saying I'm sorry doesn't fix things, but if you go to the police—and I think you should—I'll back you up. I promise. I'll tell them what I saw. –Alex Kowalski

Jen and I exchange looks.

"Alex must be the guy I told you about," she says.

I nod.

"So now what?"

"I don't know," I reply. "We need to talk."

The restaurant is busy, but Jen and I find a table for two in a corner.

"I hate this," she says, rattling her teacup around on the saucer. "Every time I think about what happened, I feel so ashamed. So dirty."

I know exactly how she feels, because I feel that way too. But I don't tell her that. "It's not your fault," I say instead.

"That's not what people think."

"People will think what they want. It doesn't change anything. You didn't do anything wrong. I didn't do anything wrong. We were victims."

"Nobody cares about that. We were raped. It makes us a juicy gossip item. Nobody cares if we were victims."

"We have to make them care. Don't you see? Alex said he'd say what really happened. He saw what Ross was doing. That's a witness, Jen. That's proof."

"But that doesn't mean anyone will believe him."

"His word, your word, my word—things are looking better all the time."

"But if we go to the police, the whole world will know. It could even end up in the newspaper. We might as well tattoo *I had sex with Ross Schroeder* on our foreheads. I would just die!"

I shake my head. "You wouldn't die. Believe me, over the last couple of months there have been times I thought I would die too. Sometimes I even wanted to. But I'm still here. The staring, the gossiping, the mean notes, being alone, doubting myself—I survived it all. And if you have to, you will too. If Ross is bragging like Alex says he is, kids at school are going to find out, so you might as well accept that there's going to be gossip. You'll feel like dirt, but you won't die." I smile. "And you know what they say—what doesn't kill you makes you stronger."

"Are *you* stronger?" she says.

I think back to where my head was after Ross raped me and where it is now. I smile again. "I will be. And so will you. We just need time."

"I don't think so. Ever since it happened, I've been afraid. I'm afraid people will find out. I'm afraid of being alone. But I'm afraid of being around people too. I'm especially afraid of Ross. But not just him. All guys. I don't think I'll ever be able to trust any guy again."

I nod. "I worry about that too. But listen to me. Before…before the rape I knew there were guys like Ross. I just never thought I'd run into one. What makes this awful isn't that we had sex.

I used to look forward to my first time. I just never expected it to be against my will. I thought it would be a mutual thing with somebody I cared about, who cared about me.

"Ross has wrecked that for me. For you too. And no matter how badly we want to go back, we can't undo what happened. We can never be who we were before. That doesn't mean we have to spend the rest of our lives being scared. There are still great guys out there. But we're never going to meet them if we keep thinking like victims. We have to stop feeling guilty. We have to stop hiding. We didn't do anything wrong. We need to believe that. And we need to fight back. I say we take Ross down."

"You mean go to the police?"

"Yes."

"Oh, I don't know, Emma," says Jen. "I'm just not that brave. I want to believe what you say. I know you're probably right. But what if we lose?"

I think about that. She has a point. We could lose. Even with Alex as a witness, Ross could get off the hook, and our names will get dragged through the mud big-time.

"I think we have to take that chance," I say. And I realize I finally mean it. "Otherwise, nothing is going to change. Keeping quiet is like saying what Ross did was okay. Don't you see? If we don't fight back, guys like Ross will keep on hurting girls like us. I don't want to live the rest of my life being afraid. We need to put the blame where it belongs."

We're quiet for a couple of minutes, both of us caught up in our own thoughts. Finally Jen says, "So how do we do this then?"

I put down my tea and look her straight in the eye. "You want to take Ross down?"

She bobs her head.

"You're sure?"

She nods once more. "Yes. You're right. We have to. It's the only way I'm going to feel like me again."

"Once we start this, there will be no going back."

"I know. But like you said, there's already no going back."

I stand up, grab Jen's hand and pull her to her feet. "There's a police station on Second Avenue."

She pulls her car keys from her pocket, takes a deep breath and says, "I'll try not to speed."

Kristin Butcher is the author of several books for young readers, including *The Trouble with Liberty* and *The Hemingway Tradition* in the Soundings collection. Kristin lives in Campbell River, British Columbia.

Check out these other gripping **SOUNDINGS** from award-winning author **KRISTIN BUTCHER**

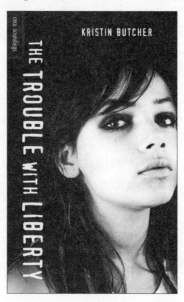

Liberty is the new girl at school, and everyone wants to be her friend. When she accuses a teacher of assault, doubts start to surface about her motives.

"Everyone who has gone to high school has met a manipulator like Liberty... This book was an absolute page-turner... Highly Recommended."
—*CM Magazine*

Zee is torn between making a statement with graffiti and making art.

"Young readers…will relate to the injustice of the adults' attitudes and actions towards Zee and his friends."
—*CM Magazine*

orca soundings

For more information on all the books
in the Orca Soundings series, please visit
orcabook.com.